The Birthday Present

Written by .rlethwaite
Illustrated by Hannah Barton

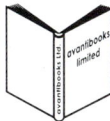

avantibooks limited

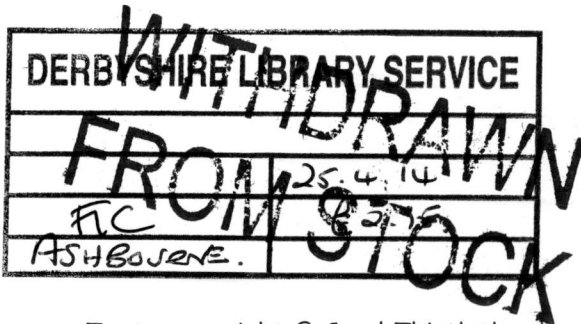

Text copyright © Carol Thistlethwaite 2006
Illustrations © Hannah Barton 2006

© Published January 2007 by
avantibooks limited

ISBN: 978 1 905309 48 1

Sanita was going to have a party.

Her son was 6 years old.

She bought spices and crushed them.

Then she mixed the spices with the food.

Today she got up at 4am. She made samosa and lots of other good things.

Granddad took Dip to school. Dip said he

would like a pet mouse for his birthday.

On the way back from school Granddad
bought a mouse from the pet shop. He
also bought a cage to put it in.

When he got home, Sanita said, 'Get that mouse out of my house!'

'But it's a birthday present for Dip,' Granddad said.

'Put it in his bedroom – and keep the cage
door shut!' Sanita said.

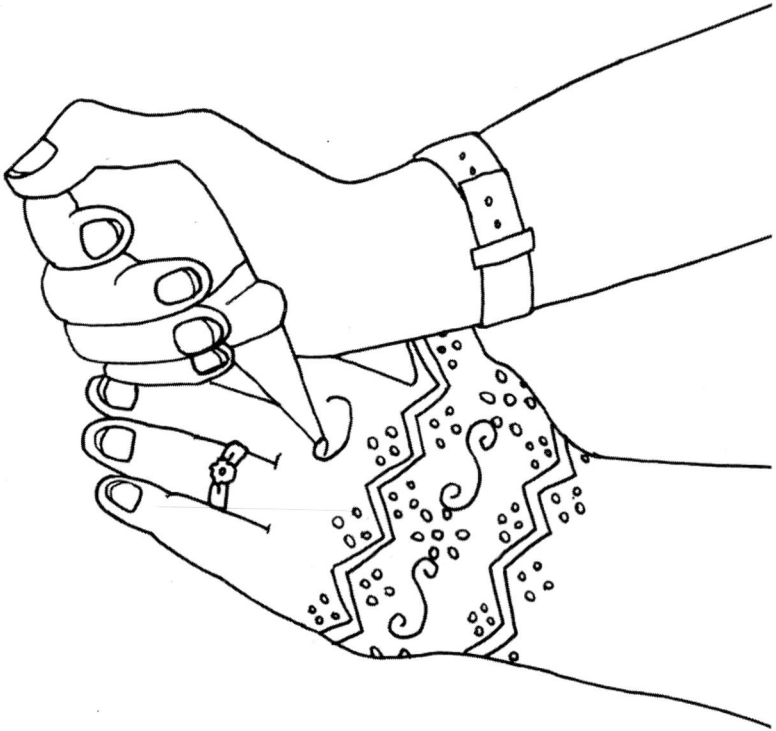

Sanita finished cooking. It was time to make herself look nice for the party, so she put henna on her hands and feet.

When Dip came home from school, Granddad gave him the mouse. 'Happy Birthday!' he said.

Dip was happy and took the mouse out of the cage.

'Put him back and shut the cage door when you finish playing with him,' Granddad said.

Soon it was time for the party, so Dip put

the mouse back in the cage but forgot to

shut the door.

It was nice to see all his aunts, uncles and cousins. Dip was happy and opened lots of presents.

'What's that in the rice?' an auntie asked.

'It's a mouse!' said Dip's uncle.

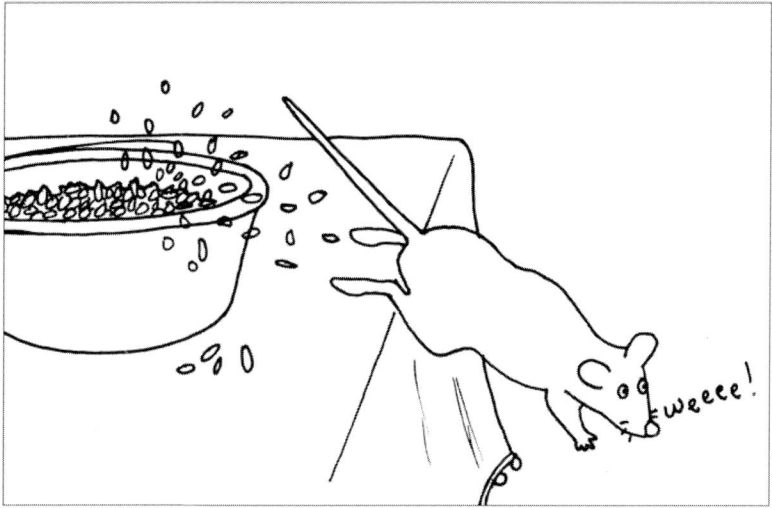

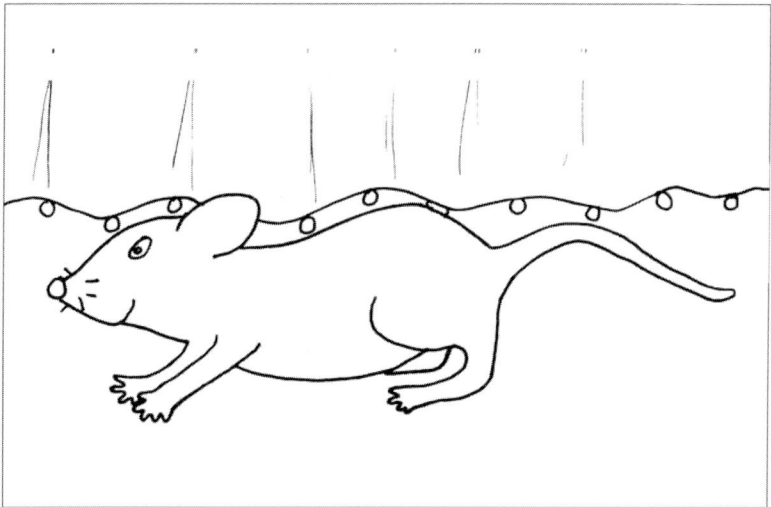

The mouse jumped out of the rice and off
the table. Then it ran along the floor.

Dip, his uncles, Dad and Granddad began
to chase the mouse.

'Don't kill him!' said Dip. 'He's my pet!'

They chased the mouse into a corner and
Dip grabbed it.

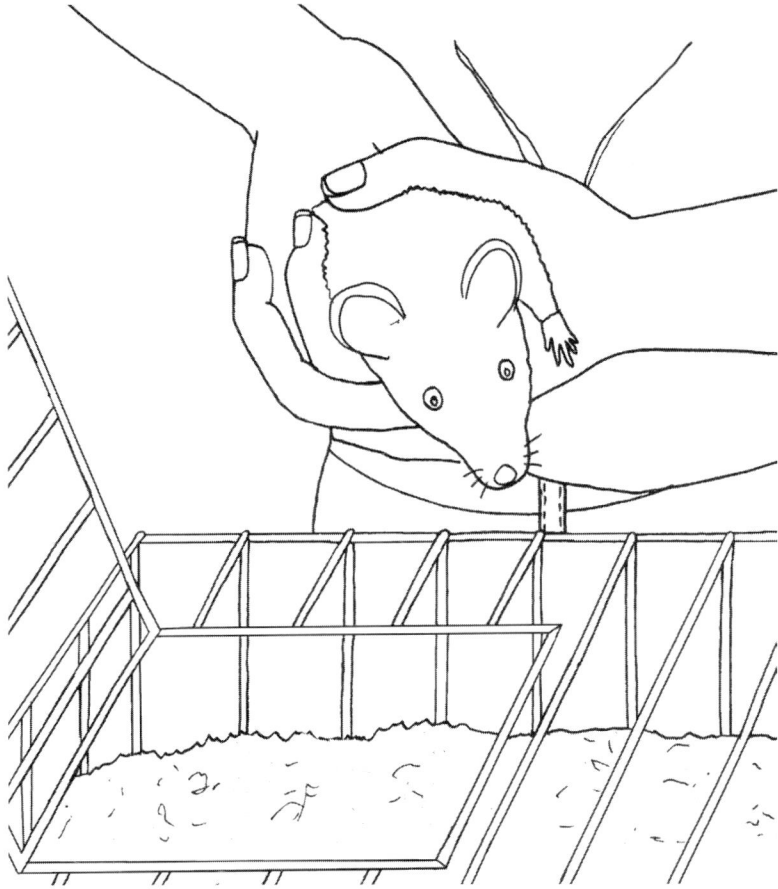

Dip put his mouse back in the cage. This time he remembered to shut the cage door.

Sanita was upset. 'No one will want to eat the food,' she said.

'Don't be upset. This is the best fun we've had at a party!' they all said.